WITHDRAWN

THIS CANDLEWICK BOOK BELONGS TO:

_____

_____

_____

First U.S. paperback edition 1992
First published in Great Britain in 1991 by Walker Books Ltd., London.

Library of Congress Cataloging-in-Publication Data

Butterworth, Nick.
My grandpa is amazing / Nick Butterworth. —1st U.S. ed.
Summary: A child describes an amazing grandfather.
ISBN 1-56402-099-1 (pbk.)
[1. Grandfathers—Fiction.] I. Title.
PZ7.B98225Myf   1992
[E]—dc20   91-58746

10

Printed in Hong Kong

The illustrations in this book were done in watercolor.

Candlewick Press
2067 Massachusetts Avenue
Cambridge, Massachusetts 02140

visit us at www.candlewick.com

MY GRANDPA IS AMAZING

by Nick Butterworth

CANDLEWICK PRESS
CAMBRIDGE, MASSACHUSETTS

My grandpa is amazing.

He builds fantastic
sand castles…

and he makes
exotic drinks...

and he's not at all
afraid of heights...

and he makes beautiful
flower arrangements...

and he's an excellent
driver…

and he knows
all about first aid…

and he's got
a great motorcycle…

and he's a terrific
dancer…

and he's very, very,
very patient…

and he invents
wonderful games.

It's great to have
a grandpa like mine.

He's amazing!

NICK BUTTERWORTH was born in 1946 and grew up in a candy shop. He has had a variety of jobs, including working as a typographer, graphic designer, magazine editor, and comic-strip illustrator. He has illustrated a number of books including *My Dad Is Awesome* and *My Mom Is Excellent*. His books *My Grandma Is Wonderful* and *My Grandpa Is Amazing* were both chosen for Fall 1992 Pick of the Lists by **American Bookseller**, which raves, "These two slim volumes are treasures. . . . The texts are simple; the illustrations are colorful, expressive, funny, and warm. [They] will appeal to all ages."